S0-BJO-753

THE TEA SQUALL
by
Ariane Dewey

GREENWILLOW BOOKS   NEW YORK

BETSEY BLIZZARD wore a buckskin dress and stuck eagle feathers in her hair.

ZIPPORINA came in lizard with a bearskin shawl.

SAL FINK smoothed her hair with bear grease and put on her calico dress. It matched the kid leather boots Mike had brought her from New Orleans.

SALLY ANN THUNDER ANN WHIRLWIND CROCKETT tied a rattlesnake belt around her bearskin robe. She bound her calfskin boots with vines to keep them up. Then she brushed her hair into tornados and put on her beehive bonnet.

FLORINDA FURY wore—well, wait and see!

KATY GOODGRIT had on a wolfskin shift with a red foxtail sash. Her hat was an eagle's nest trimmed with wolves' tails.

They looked grand!

The tales they told were tall, but all the foods served at the Tea Squall are authentic.

Library of Congress Cataloging-in-Publication Data

Dewey, Ariane.   The tea squall.
Summary: Betsey Blizzard and her friends celebrate the coming
of spring by sharing tall tales and a large tea party.
[1. Parties—Fiction]   I. Title.
PZ7.D5228Te 1988   [E]   87-14868
ISBN 0-688-07492-8   ISBN 0-688-07493-6 (lib. bdg.)

For my Mother

Betsey Blizzard's pet buzzard flew all over Kentucky delivering invitations to Sal Fink, Florinda Fury, Katy Goodgrit, Zipporina, and Sally Ann Thunder Ann Whirlwind Crockett.

Come to The Annual
Spring Tea Squall
next Saturday at
Betsey Blizzards' house.
Come early and stay late!

5

Zipporina arrived first. She clung to her canoe with one hand, and held onto a flapping, squawking wild turkey with the other.

"Zipporina, where did you get that nasty bird?" Betsey shouted.

"I snatched him up off a low branch," Zipporina called back. "He got so excited he started flying. He's towed me one hundred miles in half an hour. Throw some corn along the shore or he'll never stop!"

As soon as the turkey saw the corn he flew down to gobble it up, and Zipporina jumped ashore.

Just then a steamboat raced around the
bend. Spark-filled smoke poured from its
stacks. Sal Fink was close behind, hopping
up and down on the back of an alligator.
She shot past the steamboat and headed
for shore. Sal was as pleased with herself
as a lizard with two tails.

"That captain sure hates to be beaten,"
she gloated.

WHOOOOSH!

Sally Ann Thunder Ann Whirlwind Crockett leaped across the Ohio River. Suddenly she turned around in mid-air and headed back.

"Oh no, she's forgotten her bowie knife again," Zipporina moaned. "She never goes anywhere without that toothpick."

Sally Ann was back in a flash,

and this time she landed.

Next Florinda Fury waddled up. She was as big around as a pickle barrel.

"Hi, you-all!" she exclaimed. "Guess what just happened! My garter broke and down went my stocking. Suddenly a snake darted out of the grass and wrapped himself around my leg. Look!" And she pulled up her alligator skirt and her bearskin petticoat. A snake with its tail in its mouth was holding up her stocking.

"They should be called garter snakes," Sal said. And they have been, ever since.

"Come on inside," Betsey called. "Tea's
almost ready." They all settled down in front
of the fire. They had a lot to talk about.

"What a winter we had," said Florinda. "It was so cold that ice cream came out when I milked the cow."

"That's nothing," said Zipporina. "It was

so cold that our barn turned blue."

"I can believe that," Sally Ann said. "It was so cold down our way, that the woodpeckers never stopped hammering at stones. They were striking sparks to keep warm."

"We weren't cold," Sal Fink bragged. "I made big, thick buttermilk pancakes every night and flipped them onto our bed. Mike and I crept underneath for a cozy, warm sleep. Then we had breakfast in bed."

"It was so cold here that the flames froze on our candles," Betsey recalled. "At bedtime, we broke them off and threw them outside. The chickens thought the frozen flames were corn and ate them. The heat of their bodies melted the flames, and our hens laid hard-boiled eggs all winter."

"Fiddlesticks!" Florinda retorted. "All that fuss about a little cold."

"Well," said Sally Ann, "it was so cold that Davy and I didn't hear a thing we said to each other all winter. Our words froze as we spoke. When the weather warmed up, the words thawed out, and we had a lot of conversations to listen to."

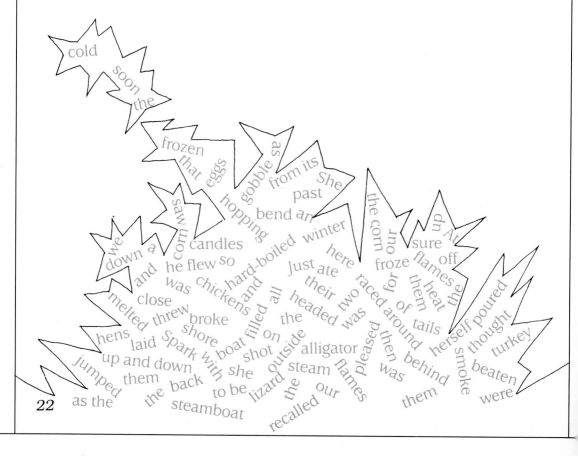

WHAM! SLAM! The door crashed open
and in rushed Katy Goodgrit.

"Come out and see what's happening,"
she panted.

Everyone but Katy ran outside.

"Nothing much going on out here now,"
Betsey said. "But Sal's alligator has turkey
feathers sticking out of his grin. Too bad,
Zipporina."

When they got back inside, Katy was
seated in the most comfortable chair.

"Doggone it, Katy, you had us jumping up
like rabbits just so you could get my favorite
seat," Florinda complained. "If this snake
had any poison in him, I'd tell him to bite
you!"

"Go ahead, I'm too tough!" Katy replied.

"Take it easy, Florinda," Betsey urged.
"Katy, you sure can interrupt a party. Why
were you so late?"

"Well, I wanted to bring you some blossoms," Katy replied, "so I climbed up a cherry tree and there I was, face to face with a wildcat. We both jumped out of the tree, and I landed on his back. The varmint took off with me hanging on.

"We'd still be traveling if we hadn't tripped over Sal Fink's alligator. Sorry about the cherry blossoms."

"Thanks anyway." Betsey beamed. "Now that we're all here, LET'S EAT!"

First she poured the tea. There was black tea, linden tea, mint tea, sassafras tea, and tea made from raspberry leaves.

Then she served:

40 kinds of corn bread
including hoecakes,

johnnycakes, ashcakes, corn oysters,

corn dodgers, corn pone, scratch backs,

and spider corn cakes with

wild honey;

187 bear bacon sandwiches
on cracklin' bread;

22 loaves of acorn bread baked with crushed
earthworms as shortening;

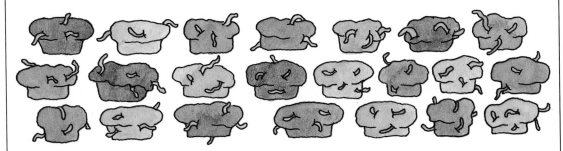

Assorted smoked snakes, eels, and lizards;

Wild rice balls with bear grease and sugar;

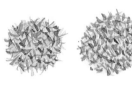

6 dozen popovers with fox grape jelly;

A gross of cinnamon buns, apple dumplings,

benne seed biscuits, and currant muffins;

Blackberry grunt
with thick cream
and blueberry slump
with nutmeg sauce;
and—

Stacks of vinegar, rhubarb, sweet potato,

and shoofly pies;

Whortleberry, suet, rutabaga, persimmon,
Indian, and hasty puddings;
2 bushels each of apple pandowdy,
gooseberry fool, and strawberry flummery;
51 bowls of sugared nuts;
and a wheelbarrow full of sand tarts,
snickerdoodles, kinkawoodles,
jolly boys, and gingersnaps.

They drank and ate, and ate and drank.

Not another word was said until the teapots

were empty and every crumb was gone.

"That was terrific," said Florinda, licking her fingers. "Next Tea Squall at my house. It'll be a job to top this one. But I'll think of something."

"See you at Florinda's," everyone
shouted. And they went home —
one way or another.